Emma Thomson's

MILTON KEYNES
COUNCIL

Library Service

This book is due *
shown. Unless reque
be renewed twice
branches listed here.   number
on the back of   card.

Bletchley (01908) 372797	
MK Central (01908) 254050	
Newport Pagnell (01908) 610933	
Olney (01234) 711474	
Stony Stratford (01908) 562562	
Westcroft (01908) 507874	
Woburn Sands (01908) 582033	
Wolverton (01908) 312812	

Children

Hodder
Children's

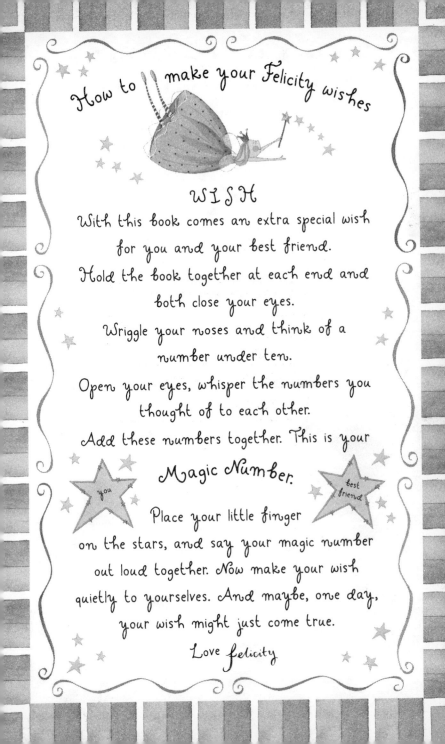

How to make your Felicity *wishes*

WISH

With this book comes an extra special wish
for you and your best friend.

Hold the book together at each end and
both close your eyes.

Wriggle your noses and think of a
number under ten.

Open your eyes, whisper the numbers you
thought of to each other.

Add these numbers together. This is your

Magic Number.

you

best friend

Place your little finger
on the stars, and say your magic number
out loud together. Now make your wish
quietly to yourselves. And maybe, one day,
your wish might just come true.

Love felicity

For Arabella Sophie and Gemma Isobel Davey,
with much love and sparkly wishes
from Auntie Emma x

Emma Thomson's
Felicity Wishes®

FELICITY WISHES
Felicity Wishes © 2000 Emma Thomson
Licensed by White Lion Publishing

Text and Illustrations © 2006 Emma Thomson

First published in Great Britain in 2006 by Hodder Children's Books

The right of Emma Thomson to be identified as the author and illustrator of this work has
been asserted by her in accordance with the Copyright, Designs and Patents Act 1988.

2

A Catalogue record for this book is available from the British Library

ISBN 9780340911983

Printed and bound in Great Britain by Bookmarque Ltd, Croydon, Surrey

The paper and board used in this paperback by Hodder Children's Books are natural recyclable
products made from wood grown in sustainable forests. The manufacturing processes
conform to the environmental regulations of the country of origin.

Hodder Children's Books
A division of Hachette Children's Books, 338 Euston Road, London NW1 3BH

CONTENTS

Perfect Polly
PAGE 7

Helping Hand
PAGE 29

Sporting Secrets
PAGE 51

Perfect Polly

Felicity Wishes' four closest friends were Holly, Polly, Daisy and Winnie. But it was Polly who was her best friend. They had known each other so long that neither of them could remember where and when they met. Felicity often thought that it was a very peculiar friendship, because she and Polly were so entirely different.

Felicity was carefree, silly and more than a little messy. Polly, on the other hand, was clever, neat and impossibly perfect in almost everything she did. Felicity longed to be like Polly, although she wasn't sure Polly wanted to be like her!

∗ ∗ ∗

"What are you up to?" Polly said to Felicity when her friend opened the door covered in paint. It was Sunday morning, and Polly had come round to see whether Felicity wanted to go out for a hot chocolate.

"Spur of the moment!" Felicity began. "I was sitting on the sofa last night just before I went to bed, wondering what my sitting room would look like if it was blue. Then I remembered I had a lovely blue crayon in the kitchen drawer."

"Tell me you didn't colour in your sitting-room wall with crayon!" exclaimed Polly, aghast.

"Well, not exactly," said Felicity, showing her friend in. "I coloured in

a small square, thought it looked
horrid, and went to bed."

Polly frowned at Felicity's overall,
dripping with bright-green paint.

"I'd forgotten all about it,"
continued Felicity, "until I
walked into the sitting
room when I got back
from shopping.

I tried to rub the crayon off, but it made such a mess that the only thing to do was paint over it, and all I had in the shed was this green, and it's a bit lumpy..." Felicity's voice trailed off.

"Oh, Felicity!" said Polly. She was well used to finding her friend in situations like this and immediately took charge. First she cleaned up the green footprints that trailed over most of the house, then, while Felicity made hot chocolate, Polly flew to Do-It-Together and picked up a large can of Sky Blue super-strength paint. They spent the whole afternoon and most of the evening painting, and by suppertime the room was entirely back to normal.

"You're perfect, Pol," said Felicity, settling down to cheese on toast in her newly painted sitting room.

"I know it sounds boring," began Polly, "but it really is much better sometimes to plan things in advance, instead of doing everything on the spur of the moment."

✳ ✳ ✳

Every Sunday evening Polly wrote an intricate diary of what she had to do that week.

MONDAY

Revise for maths test.
Make packed lunch,
    meet Holly 8 a.m.
School all day.
Maths test in the afternoon.
After-school flying club.
Soup for supper.
Bed 9 p.m., read 30 mins
History of Little Blossoming.

TUESDAY

Make packed lunch,
    meet Holly 8 a.m.
School all day.
English homework due.
Meet Felicity after school.
Sandwich for supper.
Bed 9 p.m., read 30 mins
History of Little Blossoming,
chapter 2

Polly opened the top drawer of her spotless chest of drawers, chose a fresh pair of pyjamas, had a bath and jumped in between the newly ironed sheets. It was her favourite time of the week, knowing that

everything was ready, planned and
accounted for. Polly's meticulous
arrangements meant that she never
arrived anywhere unprepared and
was always on time. She fell happily
asleep to the patter of rain on the
roof.

* * *

Holly looked at her watch:
ten past eight. It was so
unlike Polly to be late,
especially on the day
when every fairy in the
School of Nine Wishes
knew that there was an
important maths test.
And Polly always got
top marks.

SCHOOL OF
NINE WISHES

   After trying Polly
on her mobile phone
and leaving a message,
Holly decided to fly on
and meet the others.

"It's not like her," said Daisy.

"Polly's planning to beat the school record in this test," said Winnie. "I know she's been working every morning before she comes to school."

"I couldn't do anything before school except sleep!" mused Felicity.

"What do you mean?" joked Holly. "Sometimes you don't even wake up before school. I'm not the only one who's heard you snore in assembly!"

"I'd love to be more like Polly," said Felicity dreamily.

"You wouldn't be you if you were Polly!" said Holly, hugging her friend.

✳ ✳ ✳

When Polly didn't turn up at school that morning, Felicity decided to fly to her house at break-time to see if she could find out what had happened to her best friend. Felicity hadn't even reached Polly's house before she saw something that surprised her even more than Polly being late for school.

Polly lived in a valley next to a small pond. But where Polly's house should have been was a very large, very deep and very blue lake!

As Felicity flew nearer she could just make out the top storey and roof of Polly's house, peeping from under the lake.

Polly was flying waist-deep in water, dragging heavy buckets behind her.

"What in Fairy World?" called Felicity.

"A freak fairy flood!" said Polly, reaching the dry land further up the hill. "I don't know what time last night it happened, but when I woke up the whole of my downstairs and garden was submerged!"

"How awful!" said Felicity. "I hope no one was hurt."

"No, we were very lucky. Some other fairies have had their houses flooded too, but no one was injured. The water will drain away eventually, but what am I going to do in the meantime?" said Polly, with a lump in her throat.

Felicity didn't know what to say. It was usually Polly who took charge of catastrophes like this, but Polly herself never had catastrophes!

"I've phoned the fairy fire brigade," Polly said, reading her friend's thoughts, "but they said they're helping other fairies in Little Blossoming, and it may be some time before they can get here."

Felicity hugged her wet friend.

"Could you go and tell Fairy Godmother for me?" urged Polly, finally wriggling from the cuddle. "My mobile phone is waterlogged."

"I'll do better than that!" said Felicity, with a flash of inspiration. "I'll go and come back with as many fairies as I can, to help clear up this mess." And in a flutter Felicity had gone.

* * *

It took twelve fairies more than a

day and a half to clear up the water that had drenched Polly's house. It had been easy to find offers of help when it meant getting out of the maths test!

After they'd finished, Felicity stayed with Polly to help tidy up.

"This is pointless," sobbed Polly as she picked up one of her homework books, only to see it fall away from her hand in a soggy lump. "Everything is ruined! This book was full of perfectly neat history homework. Ten out of ten all the way through. And now look at it!"

Felicity put her arm around Polly's shoulder. "Why don't you come back and stay at my house for a while until everything dries out?"

Polly wasn't keen. It was in her nature to get jobs done and to be in control. She knew that to be quite happy she would have to be back at the point she had been, so cosily, on Sunday evening.

Felicity sighed as Polly determinedly pulled out a hairdryer from under a pile of wet clothes, looked at it, and then at the enormous mess of damp things that surrounded them.

"I guess you're right," said Polly.

"It will be fun!" encouraged Felicity. But Polly wasn't so sure.

* * *

It only took one day of living with Felicity before Polly wasn't perfect any more.

Even though she'd been awake in plenty of time to get to school, it had taken her twice as long to get dressed. When Polly had moved in the night before, with her single suitcase of dry clothes, Felicity had tried to find room in her wardrobe. But the only space she discovered big enough for the case was on the floor.

And it hadn't taken long before Polly's suitcase was buried under the bits and bobs that littered Felicity's room.

Even when Polly had found her suitcase, located the ironing board, got dressed and waited patiently by the front door, she could still hear Felicity's snores! And Polly couldn't bring herself to leave without her friend. Not when Felicity had been so kind to her.

* * *

The first week didn't go well. Polly found staying with Felicity increasingly frustrating, from the mess in the kitchen to her haphazard lifestyle.

"Have you ever thought of using a diary?" suggested Polly, who had already been to the fairy stationer to replace her damp one.

"I had one once..." said Felicity. "It was more of a secret diary than an everyday diary. But I put it somewhere so secret that even I couldn't find it!"

"You've been very kind in letting me stay," ventured Polly. "But I'm afraid I have to be honest, for the sake of our friendship. I can't live the way that you do. My things won't be dry for at least another week, and I was wondering if I might help you be a little more organized in that time."

It was like sparkledust to Felicity's ears. She had always aspired to be more like her friend and here, at last, was her chance.

"Yes! Yes!" said Felicity, clapping her hands. "When do we start?"

"Right now?" said Polly, glancing at the mess in the sitting room.

"Great," said Felicity, and they got stuck in straight away, cleaning, sorting and folding.

When Felicity climbed into bed that night she was snuggled between crisp clean sheets

and wearing freshly ironed pyjamas.

"I could get used to this!" Felicity said to Bertie. Polly had insisted that he must sleep on his own bed, next to Felicity's, so he didn't leave feathers on the pillow. Bertie wasn't so sure this was a good idea.

* * *

As the second week progressed, however, it was now Felicity who found living with Polly increasingly difficult – from the constant tidying to the continual organizing of their lives. They rarely seemed to do anything on the spur of the moment.

The wet things from Polly's house had been left out in the sunshine for over two weeks and when the fairy friends went to visit that Saturday, both their secret wishes had been answered. Everything was dry. They would be able to live alone in their own houses again.

"You've been a real best friend,"
said Polly, putting her key in her own
front door.

Felicity didn't answer; she was too
busy separating things into different
piles, ready to go back into the house.

"Don't bother with that now!" called out Polly to her friend. "I was thinking, why don't we pop along to the outdoor swimming pool and go for a swim? The weather is so wonderful it seems a shame to waste it tidying up."

Felicity paused, reached over to her bag and pulled out her large pink diary.

"I'd love to," she said. "But I'm afraid I can't. I've got to go shopping for tomorrow night's supper, I've got a fairy coming to tune the piano at four, and then I'm spending the rest of the afternoon doing my maths homework."

Then suddenly they both burst into fits of giggles!

"Listen to us!" spluttered Polly. "Anyone who didn't know us would think you were the sensible one."

"I am!" said Felicity indignantly "...sometimes! Let's go for that swim!"

And Felicity and Polly linked arms and flew off to the pool, leaving all the mess behind them!

Helping Hand

The School of Nine Wishes' maths
test had been postponed. Fairy
Godmother had agreed to have it on
another day, after over half Felicity's
class had been asked to help out
with a disastrous flood.

"It's great we've still got another
week before the maths test," said
Holly, opening her homework book

and scanning down her list of things to do.

"I know!" said Felicity. "If we'd had it on the day of Polly's flood, I would definitely have got bottom marks."

"And now?" asked Polly. "Have you all been revising?"

Felicity looked sheepish, Holly said she had to go, Daisy was saved by her phone ringing and Winnie pretended to be looking for something in her bag. Polly was always asking the sorts of questions her friends didn't really want to answer.

"Well, sort of," Felicity replied bravely. "I've made a revision plan!" and she handed Polly her Homework and Revising Timetable.

The list of Felicity's subjects had been lovingly lettered and coloured pink. She had divided the list up with intricate little wiggly lines and instead of writing the hours she was going to

spend on each subject she had drawn
tiny watches and clocks. The whole
thing was finished
off with a dusting
of glitter.

"It looks lovely,"
cooed Winnie,
who was peeping
over Polly's
shoulder.

"But have you
actually done
any work yet?"
asked Polly doubtfully.

"I've been too busy drawing up a
timetable!" said Felicity, as if that was
obvious.

* * *

Polly never really had to revise. She
was always so good at concentrating
in class that she rarely forgot anything
that the teachers told her.

Felicity and most of her other fairy

friends always had great fun in class, which meant they sometimes didn't listen with as much attention as they might. So they always had to revise. And in some cases, when they had been especially distracted and hadn't heard a thing the teacher had said, they had to learn completely from scratch!

"You make work for yourselves," said Polly, not unkindly.

Polly was just very sensible – she always had been – and sometimes her friends' behaviour confused her.

"If you'd listened in the first place..." she continued, as she saw her friends' eyes glaze over.

The last thing Polly wanted was to sound like a nagging teacher, but she knew there must be a way to help her friends get better marks in class and reach their full potential.

That night in bed, instead of reading

her allocated ten pages of *My Life as
a Tooth Fairy* by Amelia Crown, she
made notes in her diary about how
she might help her friends with their
maths test.

* * *

The next day was Saturday and the
five fairy friends had arranged to meet
at Sparkles Café and go shopping.

"I'll have a hot chocolate, please,"
said Holly to the waitress.

"Me too," said Polly.

"Two strawberry milkshakes for us please," asked Felicity, pointing to herself and Winnie.

"And a mint tea for me please," said Daisy.

"So," said Polly after the waitress had gone away, "how many of us want milkshakes?"

"Two," said Felicity, who was looking forward to hers.

"And how many of us are there?" Polly continued.

"Five!" said Daisy. "There's always been five of us. Why? Have you invited someone else?"

"No," said Polly mysteriously and ushered them all in close to listen to what she was about to say.

Felicity, Holly, Daisy and Winnie waited with bated breath.

"Two out of five of us want milk-shakes. Do you know what fraction of us that is?"

Felicity looked blank, Daisy looked dreamy, Holly looked horrified and Winnie looked worried!

"Two fifths! Two over five!" said Daisy triumphantly.

"Is that it? Is that what a fraction is?" said Felicity, understanding for the first time in her life.

"Yes! That's it!" said Polly.

"But fractions have always been so scary," said Winnie, who always left them till last on her test papers.

"There's no need to be scared of maths," said Polly, "and today I'm going to show you why."

Her friends couldn't help nudging each other and raising their eyes to the ceiling. They weren't as sure as Polly was that maths could be fun.

* * *

For the rest of the day Polly found interesting and intriguing ways to help her friends revise for their maths exam, without them even trying. In the wand shop she helped everyone work out what percentage of them had silver-starred wands. In Miss Fairy they all had fun working out the ratio of tops to skirts that they had taken into the changing room. And in Sticky Bun they worked out the average speed that they ate doughnuts!

By the end of the day, Polly's experiment had been a success.

She only hoped that her friends would remember it all in their test at the end of the next week.

✳ ✳ ✳

"Yesterday was fun!" said Felicity to Polly on the phone the next morning. "I was even dreaming about fractions in my sleep. I can't wait for the test next week now, to show Fairy Godmother all that I've learnt."

"That's great!" said Polly.

"I can really understand why you look forward to tests now. They're quite exciting when you know what you're doing."

Spurred on by her friend's enthusiasm, Polly suddenly had a thought.

"What about spending the afternoon at my house, with Winnie, Daisy and Holly, and I can show you all how to write out on paper what you have in your heads."

Felicity agreed readily and after she'd spoken to the others it took them less than an hour to find their maths books and fly round to Polly's house.

"I can't believe we're actually enjoying spending our weekend revising!" said Holly, who generally relaxed at weekends.

"That's because it doesn't feel like revising!" said Winnie

"Well, today is a bit more technical," said Polly. "I'm glad you all brought your books, because I'm going to show you how to make them just like mine."

Polly handed round her maths books. They were immaculate. Each sum was written with perfect and regular numbers, with no crossing out or ink blots. And, more importantly, each equation had a large red tick beside it.

Felicity looked at a page of one of her own books. She had workings-out in the margin, corrections all over the page and lots of large crosses next to most of her answers.

Holly studied Polly's book carefully.

"Wow! You don't even do any working out. You just get it right straight off!"

Polly smiled knowingly. "Well," she said quietly, "that's one of the things I was going to show you. My top tip for keeping a neat and tidy book is always to do your workings on scrap paper, not on the page. That way, when you have the answer, you can write it in; the teacher will think you are extra clever as well as very neat and give you bonus points!"

And that wasn't the only top tip Polly gave her friends. She was full of lots of useful ideas to help them understand the questions and get better marks in the test that loomed before them.

* * *

Finally the day for the test came. Fairy Godmother was shocked: she had never seen so many fairies eager to start.

With pens poised, papers on their desks, and Fairy Godmother at the front with a stopwatch, Felicity and her friends were ready to begin.

As the clock ticked, Felicity, Winnie, Daisy and Holly kept their heads down and scribbled furiously. Polly looked up for a moment and watched them all proudly. Less confident fairies began to make paper aeroplanes at the back and giggle, until Fairy Godmother caught them and told them to settle down.

Finally, with only moments to go, Polly and her friends were finished.

"If you'd like to put your pens down now and turn over your sheets, fairies, your time has run out!" said Fairy Godmother loudly as her stopwatch beeped.

"Please remain seated and do not leave until Miss Meandering has collected your papers. Everyone, that is, except Millie and Sophie. If you could wait behind, please."

Polly looked back as she left, to see Millie and Sophie getting their wands confiscated.

"That could have been you, if it hadn't had been for two fifths of us liking milkshakes!" giggled Polly.

*　*　*

The results for the test weren't posted on the school noticeboard for three days. Waiting had been excruciating for all the fairy friends. "Even if Holly,

42

Daisy, Felicity and Winnie only get a couple more points than they normally would," thought Polly to herself, "all that extra tuition would have been worth it." She knew that they often failed their maths tests.

* * *

When the big morning finally came, Winnie, Holly, Polly, Felicity and Daisy couldn't have been more surprised.

"We've all failed except Polly!" cried out Felicity, holding back her tears.

MATHS TEST RESULTS

Daisy: FAIL   Rosie: PASS
Felicity: FAIL   Sarah: PASS
Holly: FAIL   Tabitha: PASS
Polly: PASS   Mollie: FAIL
Winnie: FAIL   Amelia: PASS
Tilly: PASS   Sophie: FAIL

Miss
Amountering's
SPECIAL MATHS
CLUB
Every Tuesday
4.30pm, Room 9

"I don't understand," said Winnie, looking at Polly.

"We did everything you said!" said Daisy.

Polly felt dreadful. She didn't understand either.

"Wait here," she said. "I'm going to see Fairy Godmother. There must be some mistake."

And with a flutter she was gone.

"This is typical," said Holly, who was having the worst day of her life.

Polly was gone a long time. And when she returned it was with Fairy Godmother.

"Oh, my dear fairies," she said, pointing her wand towards a quiet room. "Step in here a moment."

"We did our best," burst out Felicity before Fairy Godmother had a chance to say anything at all.

"I know you did," said Fairy Godmother, looking kindly at Polly.

"Your friend has told me all about the extra work you put into your revision."

Winnie, Daisy, Felicity and Holly nodded eagerly.

"The thing is," said Fairy Godmother, trying hard to find exactly the right words, "most fairies are naturally talented at something. Others have to work hard at it."

All the fairy friends well understood what Fairy Godmother meant.

"Sometimes the only way to see how good someone is at something they're not naturally talented at is to watch very carefully how they do it."

"To see where they go wrong?" queried Holly.

"Exactly that!" said Fairy Godmother.

"Usually," she went on, "there are workings-out that can be given points, as well as points for actual answers themselves. Some very clever fairies, like Polly here, almost always get the answers right, so they don't need to show how they did it. But none of you others showed how you'd arrived at your answers, and I'm afraid quite a few of your answers were wrong."

Winnie opened her mouth to defend herself, but was beaten to it by Polly, who had had a revelation.

"So, sometimes," Polly said carefully, "it's better not to be perfect!"

Fairy Godmother smiled kindly at Polly and turned to face the other fairies.

"If you still have the separate sheets you did your workings-out on, I may be able to re-mark you."

Polly held her breath as Winnie, Felicity, Daisy and Holly rummaged around in their bags, until one by one they handed over crumpled sheets of paper to Fairy Godmother, covered in numbers, crossings-out and corrections.

When the new results were added
to the results list later on that week,
the fairy friends had an entirely
different reaction than the first time
they'd seen it!

"We passed!" said Felicity, squealing.
"All of us! We passed!" she said again,
barely able to believe it.

Polly was overjoyed. "Well, this calls for a proper celebration!" she said. "With five fifths of double-choc ice cream!"

And everyone agreed.

The sum of all your friends

makes one whole heart

Sporting Secrets

Fairy Godmother had always kept a special eye on Polly, ever since she first started at the School of Nine Wishes. She thought that one day she would make an excellent Head Fairy Girl.

Polly was naturally gifted in so many areas. She was a warm, generous and caring friend. She had a strong sense of right and wrong, and she was incredibly clever, without being conceited about it.

Polly wanted to become a tooth fairy when she graduated with double wings. She knew that to realize her dream would mean a lot of hard work. But with every exam she passed Polly knew she was flying a little bit closer to making that dream come true.

When Fairy Godmother was asked who she would recommend to represent the school, she knew in a flutter who it would be.

* * *

"Where's Polly?" Felicity Wishes asked her fairy friends Daisy, Winnie and Holly. "It's most unlike her to miss a lesson."

"Fairy Godmother came into class just before you got here and asked her to spend five minutes in her office," said Winnie.

"I hope she hasn't done anything

wrong," said Felicity nervously. Then she remembered it was Polly they were talking about. "Actually, it's more likely she's being awarded more gold stars for her history homework!"

* * *

When Polly returned to class, though, she didn't have any gold stars and she was acting very mysteriously.

"I can't say anything," she said when her friends quizzed her about what Fairy Godmother had said.

"Whisper it, no one will hear!" urged Felicity, who was never any good at keeping secrets.

"If I told you it would ruin the surprise for everyone. Only Fairy Godmother and I know about it," said Polly, beaming.

"What is it!" whined Holly.

"You'll find out soon. But until then you might have to pretend you haven't seen certain things!"

Felicity and her friends were baffled. They always shared each other's secrets and it was torture being kept in the dark. They loved gossiping almost as much as they loved secrets.

"Couldn't you just tell me?" pleaded Felicity after class. "I promise I won't tell anyone else. You know you can trust me."

"I'm sorry, Felicity, I can't," said Polly firmly. "You'll find out with all the others… just wait and see!"

* * *

Over the next few days Polly began to behave very strangely indeed. She normally allowed some time in her day for fun with Felicity and her friends, but suddenly she didn't have time for fun any more. She began to miss out on lunchtime and break, and go to the library instead. As Felicity, Holly, Daisy and Winnie were sharing their lunch under the Large Oak Tree they could see Polly through the library window, hard at work. But whenever they went to visit Polly or take her some lunch, she would cover the computer screen with her arms.

It was exciting, but it was also tiring work for Polly. She always tried her absolute best to be perfect at everything she did, whether it was something tiny like mowing her lawn in ultra-straight lines, or something big, like this, that she would be remembered for in Fairy World forever.

The Fairy World School Games were held every seven years. The last time they'd been held Polly hadn't even been at school, but she remembered watching them on television. Everyone knew that this year the Land of Friends was hosting the event, but very few fairies knew that Little Blossoming, and more importantly, the School of Nine Wishes, was where most of the competitions would take place. There was a tremendous amount to organize and for the last few months Fairy Godmother had been doing it all herself. She was relieved and pleased finally to be given permission by the official organizers to enrol one other helper – Polly!

Private and confidential – TOP SECRET

Fairy World School Games – to be held at the School of Nine Wishes

Countdown to the day – 289 days to go

Categories	running, jumping, flying, swimming, wishing, throwing, gymnastics
Launch party	catering, representative's speech, wand of fire, song
Events	judges, location, prizes
Competitors	accommodation, team uniforms, catering
Press	official photographers, briefing room, results

Polly had accepted the honour of carrying the wand of fire without a moment's hesitation. Every Fairy World School Games began with this very special ceremony. One specially chosen fairy from the host country would fly, with a lighted wand, to light the wands of all the other fairies representing their countries. And when all the wands were alight they would come together on the stage while a welcome speech was made and everyone sang a song to begin the games. Afterwards there would be an enormous party.

What Polly hadn't realized until much later in her talks with Fairy Godmother was that it would be up to her to write and perform the opening speech and song. There was so much to do and to get exactly right.

First she had to learn to fly carrying a lighted wand without singeing her wings or setting light to her crown. But it was impossible to put in the daily practice she would need without raising her friends' suspicions. So instead she had decided to concentrate on developing her balance, strength and ability to fly in a straight line.

* * *

When Felicity, Winnie, Holly and Daisy first saw Polly balancing a cup of tea on her wand, they couldn't contain their giggles.

"What in Fairy World are you doing?" they burst out all at once.

"It's part of the secret I was telling you about yesterday!" said Polly.

"You can't fly all the way to school like that," said Holly, looking at Polly as if she was mad.

"I have to!" said Polly. "It's the only way to learn. I've got less than a month to learn to fly like this, with my eyes closed and without spilling a drop!"

"Is this part of your training to become a tooth fairy?" asked Felicity, thinking she'd discovered part of Polly's secret. "You'd have to be able to fly in a straight line with a coin and a tooth to be a professional tooth fairy, which doesn't sound easy."

Polly was afraid to give her friends any hints at the secret in case they guessed, so instead she just shrugged her shoulders and said, "Maybe. You'll just have to wait and see!"

"We could help you!" said Winnie, steadying Polly's saucer as she fluttered above them.

But Polly just shrugged a secret shrug.

✳ ✳ ✳

The second part of Polly's task was to write the speech, which was harder than she first thought. Not only did she have to welcome each and every country in their own language, but she also had to talk about what hosting the Fairy World School Games would mean to the School of Nine Wishes.

When Daisy caught Polly muttering
something to herself in a language
that seemed familiar she couldn't help
but be intrigued.

"What did you just say?" she said,
wondering if she was hearing things.

Polly looked sheepish. She hadn't
realized that she'd even said anything
out loud.

"Um… nothing!" she said firmly.

"It sounded like the old language
that's used to name plants," persisted
Daisy, who knew most languages had
derived from that one.

Polly shrugged.

"Is it something to do with your
secret with Fairy Godmother?" pressed
Daisy. "I could help you if I knew."

"Maybe…" said Polly helplessly,
longing for some help. "You'll just
have to wait and see."

* * *

The final part of Polly's task was to write a song. Polly could just about manage both the other parts of her task by herself, but the song was a different matter. No matter how naturally talented she was at most things, music was one thing she really had to work at. Together with her friends she had made up hundreds of dance routines and songs they had sung into hairbrushes in front of the mirror. But this was different. This was real and it had to be sung not in a bedroom, but on a stage in front of hundreds of other fairies.

It was this that Polly sat in the library every lunchtime trying unsuccessfully to work out. She was finding it impossible without her friends.

"Are you OK?" whispered Felicity, sitting down beside Polly in the library at break-time. She had noticed that her best friend's wings had appeared to be under a lot of strain recently.

"I'm fine," said Polly in a whisper, trying to hold back the tears.

"No, you're not!" said Felicity, getting up and beckoning her friend to leave the library.

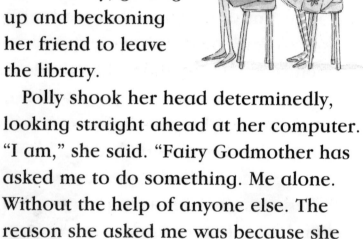

Polly shook her head determinedly, looking straight ahead at her computer. "I am," she said. "Fairy Godmother has asked me to do something. Me alone. Without the help of anyone else. The reason she asked me was because she knew I could do it. I don't want to let her down."

"I don't want to see you unhappy," said Felicity kindly. "I know you can't tell me what you're up to, and I won't ask, but you know I'm here if you need me."

"Shhhhhhh!" said Miss Page, the

SILENCE

librarian, pointing her wand at the fairy friends.

Gravely Polly nodded to Felicity.

"You can't be perfect all the time, Pol," whispered Felicity, and she gave her friend a big hug before she got up to leave.

Felicity didn't like to see her best friend so down in the dumps, so she decided to pay Fairy Godmother a secret visit...

* * *

The next day Fairy Godmother called Polly for a special update meeting. Polly felt dreadful. She was doing well with her flying practice to carry the lighted wand, she was even making some progress learning all the different languages, but she was still stuck on the song. She didn't know what she was going to say.

Luckily she didn't have to say

anything. It was Fairy Godmother
who spoke first.

"My dear Polly," she said kindly, "do
sit down."

Nervously Polly sat clutching the
pile of paper that contained her draft
opening speech.

"I don't know about you," Fairy
Godmother continued, "but I've been
finding all of this a little wearing on
my wings to do by myself."

Polly didn't know whether to agree

or not. She really didn't want to fail Fairy Godmother.

"It's been OK," said Polly, not being entirely honest.

"Oh, you are good," said Fairy Godmother. "I'm afraid I can't say the same." And she opened up a secret drawer to show Polly all the paper-work she had been sorting out.

"However much I didn't want to let down the Fairy World School Games organizers, I just couldn't do this by myself any more. So I applied for special permission to increase the team and let more fairies into the secret."

A wave of relief washed over Polly's wings and she nearly dropped her papers.

"The letter came this morning," continued Fairy Godmother. "They have allowed us each to have four assistants, but they must be sworn to secrecy in the same way we have been. We can't allow the newspapers to know about this before the school."

Polly nearly whooped with delight. "That's wonderful news!" she said, beaming.

Fairy Godmother smiled a knowing smile.

"Fairy Godmother, you are the most

perfect fairy I know," said Polly, jumping for joy. "You have shown me the most perfect thing I can do now is to get help and not try to do it all by myself. And I know exactly who I'm going to ask!"

"I think I know too," said Fairy Godmother, opening her office door to four smiling fairies.

"I'll let you into a secret," said Felicity, giving her best friend a hug "With friends beside you, everything can be perfect!"

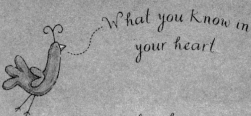

What you know in
your heart

can be shown
by someone
you love

Emma Thomson's
Felicity Wishes

Felicity offers

some fashion advice

to Holly in

Holly's Hideaway

Fashion Folly

Holly wasn't a natural fairy. She had to work hard at doing all the things a good fairy should. It wasn't that she didn't want to be a good fairy... although she did sometimes struggle with the effort it took!

But there was one aspect of being a fairy that Holly excelled in: fashion!

Holly was the trendiest fairy in the whole of Little Blossoming. She was always ahead of the latest fashions, always had the most up-to-date wardrobe, and always, always looked amazing!

And it was no secret that Holly wanted to be a Christmas Tree fairy when she graduated. She loved to be the centre of attention – and sitting on top of a tree looking pretty would certainly be suited to her idle nature!

"What do you mean, you've forgotten your flying wings?" said Miss Speeding, the school flying mistress.

"They're so uncomfortable," moaned Holly, who was not especially bothered about learning to loop-the-loop. "Can't I fly in these instead?" She spun round and showed Miss Speeding the top fairy fashion accessories of the moment.

"You know perfectly well, Holly, that those wings are not for professional flying. These flimsy things may look lovely," she tapped them disapprovingly with her wand, "but practical they are not. I'm surprised you even made it into school this morning without falling from the sky."

Holly quickly covered her dirty knees with her bag. The last thing she wanted was for Miss Speeding to know that she had indeed fallen from the sky that morning.

Miss Speeding looked thoughtful for a moment and, without another word, headed back to her office.

"I think I've got out of the flying lesson!" said Holly gleefully to Felicity Wishes. "I should forget my flying wings more often!"

Felicity shook her head. "I can't believe you want to get out of it. It's the most amazing fairy feeling in the world, being able to swoop and fly like a bird."

"Oh, I like flying, I just don't like all the physical exertion and getting all hot and bothered," said Holly, who'd always been more than a little lazy. "It always ruins my hairdo."

"Right!" said Miss Speeding, returning to address Holly.

"I've got some homework I can be getting on with until the flying class is finished," offered Holly.

"Oh, there'll be no need for that," said Miss Speeding. "I found you these." And from behind her back Miss Speeding produced the most horrid, ugly old wings Holly had ever seen!

"Chop, chop!" said Miss Speeding. "Don't stand there gawping. Get changed quickly and then fly and join the others on the right wing of the school roof."

Felicity stared at the tatty old wings and then at her fashion-conscious friend. "Don't worry, Holly. I'm sure it will be fine," she said, trying to sound confident.

* * *

Two days later, Holly still hadn't got over the indignity of it. She was one of those fairies who was very concerned about what everyone else thought.

"You're going to have to take off those dark glasses at some time or other," said Felicity, disconcerted at not being able to see her friend's eyes.

"I can't," sobbed Holly. "I'm too embarrassed. No one's ever going to forget what a fool I looked in flying class on Monday."

"Oh, Holly," said Polly. "You're exaggerating. No one even noticed your wings in flying class."

"What wings?" asked Daisy, trying to make her friend feel better.

But just as she said it two novice fairies from the year below walked past the fairy friends, pointed at Holly and then started to giggle uncontrollably.

"You were saying?" said Holly, distraught.

✳ ✳ ✳

Felicity didn't know what to say. Instead, she started thinking. She thought so hard and for so long that it wasn't until lunchtime the next day that she finally caught up with Holly underneath the Large Oak Tree in the middle of the playing field.

"I don't know how to say this without hurting your feelings," began Felicity, determined to be as honest as she could.

"Well, maybe you shouldn't say anything," said Holly, who was sure other fairies were still laughing at her.

"I just want to help," offered Felicity. "Look," she said softly, peeping over her friend's sunglasses, "I think sometimes you worry too much about what other fairies think. The most important thing is what *you* think, on the inside. Do you understand what I mean?"

Holly didn't. All she knew was that

she felt a fool and nothing she could imagine would change that.

"I've had an idea," said Felicity. "It's going to be hard. But you are the only fairy I know who can make it work."

Holly sighed. She knew Felicity's ideas didn't always go to plan. Short of Felicity turning her into another fairy or giving her a one-way ticket to another country halfway around Fairy World, Holly couldn't think of anything that could make her feel better.

"Will it make the giggling and teasing stop?" she asked.

"It will!" said Felicity resolutely.

Holly looked unconvinced. "Don't tell me. You've made a sparkledust concoction in chemistry to make everyone in the school forget they saw the trendiest fairy in Little Blossoming looking like a walking dustbin!"

Felicity winced. "No," she said patiently. "It's not sparkledust exactly. But it is a magic wish. And for you to make it work you're going to have to use your best acting skills."

"Acting skills?" said Holly. She took off her glasses and swished her hair dramatically. "I've always loved drama, you know that."

In the blink of an eye, Holly slipped into the role she'd played in the school pantomime – Cinderella. Felicity giggled as Holly pretended to sweep the floor around her and wipe her tired brow.

"What's the role?" said Holly, coming back to reality.

Felicity paused. "The role is the most demanding one you've ever done!" she said, rummaging around in her bag. "I'd like you to wear these all day, every day for seven days and nights... and love it!"

And Felicity pulled out the horrid old wings Miss Speeding had made Holly wear in flying class just a few days before.

"Are you crazy?" said Holly, thinking it was some kind of joke.

"I said it would be a demanding role!" said Felicity. "Just think how much acting talent it will take to pull it off convincingly!"

Holly was aghast that her friend actually seemed to be serious.

"But of course," said Felicity, "if you don't think you're talented enough…"

"Talented?" said Holly. "You know I'm the best fairy at drama in the whole school!"

"Then you should have no problem doing this," said Felicity, holding out the wings.

Holly poked them with the end of her wand, a disgusted look on her face. "I don't see what possible good it would do except to make people laugh at me even more."

"Well," said Felicity, taking Holly's sparkling trendy wings off her and handing her the old tatty ones, "that depends. If you're as good an actress as you think you are then I can guarantee something magical will happen."

Holly still looked unsure.

"Trust me," said Felicity. "I'm a fairy!"

* * *

Holly had nothing to lose. She knew that she couldn't carry on hiding behind dark glasses forever, and she knew that she could trust Felicity to have her best interests at heart.

With a heavy sigh, Holly pulled on the horrid wings as though they were the most beautiful, exclusive pair of wings she had ever owned. She straightened her shoulders, beamed an enormous smile, and winked at Felicity.

"All the best actresses are true professionals," she called out as she flew into school with her head held high.

Just as Felicity had warned, it was the hardest role Holly had ever had to play. Harder than the time she'd acted the lead in the school Christmas play, harder than the time she'd gone on at the last minute in the talent competition… and even harder than the time she'd had to tell a white lie to Fairy Godmother to get her friends out of trouble.

* * *

"Nice wings!" giggled Daisy and Winnie as Holly sat down beside them in class.

"Yes," said Holly, to the surprise of everyone watching. "They are, aren't they! After Miss Speeding made me wear them the other day I realized they were actually far more practical than the usual silly fashion nonsense I wear."

"You can't be serious," said Polly, who had fluttered over from the other side of the room. "They're horrid, and full of holes!"

"I'm perfectly serious," said Holly loudly. "They may have holes, but they certainly have more character than the wings everyone gets from Wings and Things. No one else in the school has a pair of wings like these!" she said with pride, getting up on to her chair and spinning around on the spot for the whole class to see.

Felicity beamed at her friend. Holly really was a great actress.

"Oh," said Polly. "I thought you were wearing them for a joke or something."

"No joke!" said Holly, as she

watched her acting skills convince the fairies around her. "These wings are currently my favourite accessory!"

✳ ✳ ✳

As the week progressed, Felicity watched from the sidelines as fairies' attitudes towards Holly and her wings changed.

Read the rest of

Emma Thomson's

felicity Wishes

Holly's Hideaway

to find out whether
Felicity can work her
friendship magic!

If you enjoyed this book, why not try another of these fantastic story collections?

1 Designer Drama

2 Star Surprise

3 Clutter Clean-out

4 Newspaper Nerves

5 Enchanted Escape

6 Whispering Wishes

7 Sensational Secrets

8 Friends Forever

9 Happy Hobbies

10 Party Pickle

11 Wand Wishes

12 Dancing Dreams

Fashion Fiasco

Spooky Sleepover

Pink Paradise

Dreamy Daisy

Spectacular Skies

Perfect Polly

20

Holly's Hideaway

19

Winnie's Wonderland

21

Fairy Fun

Look out for these three special editions

Summer Sunshine

Christmas Calamity

Winter Wishes

SEE YOUR FRIENDSHIP LETTER HERE!

Write in and tell us all about your best friend, and you could see your letter published in one of the Felicity Wishes books.

Please send in your letter, including your name and age, with a stamped self-addressed envelope to:

Felicity Wishes Friendship Competition

Hodder Children's Books, 338 Euston Road, London NW1 3BH

Australian readers should write to...
Hachette Children's Books
Level 17/207 Kent Street, Sydney, NSW 2000, Australia

New Zealand readers should write to...
Hachette Children's Books
PO Box 100-749 North Shore Mail Centre, Auckland, New Zealand

Closing date is 30 April 2007

ALL ENTRIES MUST BE SIGNED BY A PARENT OR GUARDIAN.
TO BE ELIGIBLE ENTRANTS MUST BE UNDER 13 YEARS.

For full terms and conditions visit www.felicitywishes.net/terms

Friends of Felicity

My Name is Monifa
age 9 years

A am nominating my best friend Alexis Palmer. She is verry funny. When I am upset she tries to help me in any way she can. We look out for each other. Alexis likes me for who I am and likes me just as much as she likes anyone else. We tell each other everything. A good friendship is never tell lies and be honest with each other. We like the same things our best hobby is netball we play it at school. We met each other when we were five in the same class. Over many years our friendship has grown much stronger. BFF stands for Best friends for life and we always will be.

from Monifa

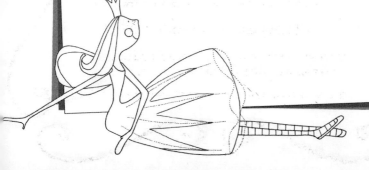

WIN FELICITY WISHES PRIZES!

From January 2006, there will
be a Felicity Wishes fiction book
publishing each month (in Australia
and New Zealand publishing from
April 2006) with a different
sticker on each cover. Collect
all twelve stickers and stick
them on the collectors' card which
you'll find in *Dancing Dreams* or
download from www.felicitywishes.net

Send in your completed card to the relevant
address below and you'll be entered into a
grand prize draw to receive a Felicity Wishes prize.*

Felicity Wishes Collectors' Competition

Hodder Children's Books, 338 Euston Road, London NW1 3BH

Australian readers should write to...
Hachette Children's Books
Level 17/207 Kent Street, Sydney, NSW 2000, Australia

New Zealand readers should write to...
Hachette Children's Books
PO Box 100-749 North Shore Mail Centre, Auckland, New Zealand

*A draw to pick 50 winners each month
will take place from January 2007 – 30th June 2007.

For full terms and conditions visit www.felicitywishes.net/terms

WOULD YOU LIKE TO BE A FRIEND OF FELICITY?

Felicity Wishes has her very own website,
filled with lots of sparkly fairy fun and information
about Felicity Wishes and all her fairy friends.

Just visit:

www.felicitywishes.net

to find out all about
Felicity's books,
sign up to
competitions,
quizzes and
special offers.

And if you want
to show how much
you love your friends,
you can even send
them a Felicity e-card
for free. It will truly
brighten up their day!

For full terms and conditions visit www.felicitywishes.net/terms